Sunset Shimmer's Time to Shine

by Perdita Finn

Little, Brown and Company
New York ✳ Boston

Little, Brown and Company

Hachette Book Group
1290 Avenue of the Americas, New York, NY 10104
Visit us at lb-kids.com

Little, Brown and Company is a division of Hachette Book Group, Inc.
The Little, Brown name and logo are trademarks of Hachette Book Group, Inc.

The publisher is not responsible for websites (or their content)
that are not owned by the publisher.

First Edition: May 2015

Library of Congress Control Number: 2014960212

ISBN 978-0-316-41079-3

10 9 8 7 6 5 4 3 2 1

RRD-C

Printed in the United States of America

For Leah and Joanna—
my first and bestest pony fans

CONTENTS

✶ ✶ ✶

CHAPTER

1

A Ray of Sunshine... Not

★ ★ ★

The hallways of Canterlot High were bustling with students on their way to class. Kids were calling out to their friends, scribbling down last-minute answers on their homework, and grabbing their books from their lockers. The first-period bell was just about to ring.

"Howdy, gals!" Applejack called out,

bounding over to her friends as they headed to chemistry class. "Ready for the big test?"

"I'm nervous," admitted Fluttershy, biting her lip.

Rainbow Dash gave her an encouraging smile. "Just remember what we studied together and you'll do great! It's all about practice, after all. That's what counts. We've done the drills and we're ready for the game. Right?"

"That's right," agreed Pinkie Pie. "It's just like cooking. A bit of this, a bit of that, and, *boom*, cupcakes!" She giggled.

"Slow down, partner," said Applejack. "We don't want any explosions if we can help it, but you've got the basic idea, that's true. You throw a lot of things together and all of a sudden you have somethin' brand-new, just like magic."

Fluttershy took a deep breath.

"Besides," said Rarity, reassuringly putting her arm through her friend's, "if we can make real magic happen when we play music together in our band, how hard can a school test be?"

Fluttershy smiled. "Maybe we can start singing together and pony up during the exam!"

"Whoa!" said Applejack. "That's only for special occasions. We all know that."

The girls nodded, suddenly serious. Whenever they played music together in their band, the Sonic Rainbooms, they would grow cute ears, flowing manes, and long, flouncing tails. It had all started when Twilight Sparkle, the Princess of Friendship, visited their high school from Equestria and left behind a bit of enchantment from the world of magical ponies.

"Time for class! Time for class!" Vice Principal Luna was striding down the hallway, clapping her hands.

"Okay, this is it." Fluttershy gulped.

Flash Sentry raced past the girls into the chemistry classroom, his face buried in his notes. DJ Pon-3 turned off her music and took off her earphones. Trixie flounced past and took a seat in a front-row desk.

"Hey, where's Sunset Shimmer?" asked Rainbow Dash, looking around.

"She's going to be late," said Applejack.

"There she is!" Rarity pointed down the hallway, where a girl was slipping through the main doors of the school just before they closed. As if she didn't have a care in the world, Sunset Shimmer strolled to her locker, gave her pretty red-gold hair a quick brush, and grabbed a single sharp pencil. Her friends were all waiting for her outside the classroom.

"We missed you last night at our study session," said Applejack.

"Are you worried about the test?" whispered Fluttershy to her friend.

"No," answered Sunset Shimmer honestly. "You just have to memorize the formulas and the reactions and the periodic table and all the elements, and be able to predict reactions, and check your answers, and do all the math without making a mistake. That's all."

The girls' eyes widened. Rarity gulped.

"We did so many practice problems together last night," said Rainbow Dash reassuringly.

"Chemistry isn't very hard for me,"

apologized Sunset Shimmer when she realized she had scared her friends. "Not after studying magic in Equestria."

"We made cookies, too, last night!" announced Pinkie Pie, changing the subject. "After all, what's a study session without a little baking?"

Sunset Shimmer's face fell. "You made cookies?"

The girls nodded together.

"We saved you some," said Fluttershy. "Next time you should come. I know you don't need any help with schoolwork, but we love hanging out with you."

"And, honestly, we could use a little help," said Applejack with a wink.

The bell rang, and the last stragglers scurried past the girls to class. The girls slipped into their seats, and Sunset Shimmer took her place in the last row. Rarity noticed that she was frowning.

"Don't worry about the test," she said. "You're so smart. You always do great."

But it wasn't chemistry that Sunset Shimmer was worried about. When she'd been invited to the study session, she hadn't seen any reason to bother going. But she'd only been thinking about herself. She hadn't realized that maybe she could help the others practice, that maybe they would have fun together in the midst of the studying and she could be part of it. She sighed. Another day as a human girl at Canterlot High was about to begin and already she had made a mistake about friendship.

CHAPTER

2

Storm on the Horizon

★ ★ ★

Sunset Shimmer put down her pencil. She was done. Before anyone else in the class. As usual. She handed in her test and went back to her desk.

When she first came to Canterlot High, she had been determined to succeed as a human girl, and she kind of had. In a matter of weeks, she had become the most popular girl in the whole school. She'd gotten herself elected as the princess of the Fall Formal, and the handsome Flash Sentry had been her boyfriend. Of course, she'd also stolen a magic crown from Equestria and turned herself into a world-conquering she-demon, but after Twilight Sparkle defeated her, everyone somehow forgave her. And when the evil Sirens tried to sow disharmony at Canterlot High, Sunset Shimmer took the opportunity to show everyone that she could be part of the team. Still, the day-to-day challenges of being an ordinary friend were sometimes harder than anything she had ever done before.

Her classes were a breeze. No student had been better than her in Equestria, except for Twilight Sparkle. Mastering magic was a lot more complicated than math and science and social studies and English—that was for sure. She twirled her hair around her pencil and looked around the room. Everyone was hunched over the test, working hard.

Sunset Shimmer took a notebook filled with numbers and symbols from her backpack. She was trying to figure out a formula to explain how the magic of this world worked. If you took five girls—six girls, including her—and they could each play seven different notes, how did that add up to magic? Of course, each girl played a different instrument and they sang lots of different songs and you probably had to factor in the words of those songs, and the girls' movements, and possibly even what they were wearing. . . . It was such a complicated problem. Six plus seven plus who-knows-what equaled everyone ponying up! If only someone could help her think about this. She looked around the classroom.

Fluttershy was nervously biting her lip. Rainbow Dash was erasing an answer. Rarity was meticulously checking over the questions. Pinkie Pie was staring out the window and humming before she remembered the test and furiously scribbled again. The girls seemed so, well, ordinary, and yet when they played music together, the magic happened. How did it work?

If only Twilight Sparkle were here to help her solve this magic puzzle. That's when Sunset Shimmer remembered her special journal that let her send messages back and forth to her pony friend in Equestria. She took out her journal and dashed off a note to Twilight Sparkle.

Dear Twilight Sparkle, she wrote. *Sometimes I'm a little jealous that you get to come to Canterlot High for magical adventures and I have to be here every day figuring out how to be a real girl and a real friend. When I was studying conjuring and spells with Princess Celestia, I always understood my purpose, but now I don't know what I'm doing and I don't really know why I'm here.*

Sunset Shimmer closed the cover of the journal. She never knew when Twilight Sparkle would write her back, but at some point, she'd open the magic book and find a letter from her friend on one of the pages.

She glanced at the clock. Class was almost over, and kids were scrambling to complete the test.

"That's it. Time's up," announced the teacher.

The bell rang.

"That wasn't as hard as I thought!" said Fluttershy when the girls were out in the hall.

"That's because you practiced!" said Rainbow Dash.

"We did it! We did it! We did it!" Pinkie Pie gushed. "I say we celebrate with a sleepover party at my house tonight."

"Yay!" shouted all the girls together.

"Yay," said Sunset Shimmer. She was so happy to have a chance to join her friends, especially after missing out on the study session.

"Shall we come over right after school?" she asked eagerly.

"Can't miss soccer practice," said Rainbow Dash. "But I'll see you afterward."

"Me too," added Rarity. "I'm working on

some costumes for the school play with the drama club, but I can be there for dinner."

"I've got to write up some stories for the newspaper before I'm free," said Applejack.

"I've got to drop in at the animal shelter," Fluttershy said. "For a little while anyway."

"And I've got the yearbook and student council and glee club and"—Pinkie Pie took a big breath—"I've got to decorate for our party tonight and order the pizza. What are you doing this afternoon, Sunset Shimmer?"

The girls were busy with so many activities, but Sunset Shimmer wasn't yet a part of any club or team at Canterlot High. What she wanted to do more than anything when school was over was study magic. She thought of the books of spells and diagrams and formulas waiting for her at home.

Where did magic come from? How did it work? That's what she wanted to know. But that wasn't something she was talented at the way Rainbow Dash was good at sports or Rarity excelled at fashion.

The girls were looking at her expectantly.

Sunset Shimmer brushed a curl off her forehead. "I have to...um...study magic," she admitted to her friends, worried they might make fun of her.

The girls' eyes widened.

"Of course."

"Yes, yes."

"Tell Twilight Sparkle we said hello if you talk to her."

"Twilight Sparkle?" Flash Sentry was passing by them in the hallway and had overheard them. "Is she coming back to Canterlot High?"

"Not for a long time," sighed Sunset Shimmer, who missed her, too.

Flash Sentry's shoulders slumped as he headed to his next class.

"He really misses her," said Rarity.

"We all do," said Applejack. "She's one fine filly. If it hadn't been for her, who knows what those Sirens would have done?"

"I helped, too," said Sunset Shimmer, wanting to remind her friends about her moment of glory. But as soon as the words were out of her mouth, she knew she'd hit the wrong note. It sounded like she was bragging.

"Of course you helped," said Rainbow Dash. "It was teamwork all the way!"

The girls chattered cheerfully on their way to math class, but Sunset Shimmer hung back. They would all be busy this afternoon. She wished there was a club for magic at the school. She wished there was someone who wanted to learn about it with her. The only problem with studying all the time was that it could be lonely. She glanced in her journal to see if there was any word from Twilight Sparkle. Nothing yet.

With her nose in her book, she nearly bumped into Trixie.

"Watch where you are going! The Great and Powerful Trixie does not like to have her feet stepped on!" Trixie stomped off, her nose in the air.

Sunset Shimmer tucked the journal into her bag. Back to the problem at hand. How did the magic in this world work? There had to be a formula, and she was going to figure it out. She just needed to think about all the different things that went into it—the notes, the music, the instruments. She sighed, thinking about the long afternoon alone ahead. She hoped she'd hear from Twilight Sparkle soon. She really needed her—not just to help figure out magic but because she needed her friendship.

Lightning Strikes

✶ ✶ ✶

After glee club, Pinkie Pie skipped home to get ready for the slumber party. There were snacks to prepare and pizzas to order and balloons to blow up. She'd bought special little pillows that she decorated with ribbons and decals for each of her friends. Rainbow Dash's had a soccer ball and Fluttershy's a bunny and Applejack's a lasso and Rarity's a high-heeled shoe, but she hadn't known what to put on Sunset Shimmer's. What was it Sunset Shimmer liked to do most of all? In the end, she chose a beautiful decal of a setting sun with its rays spreading up toward the clouds—shimmering.

"There," she squealed, looking around her bedroom. "Almost ready."

Applejack was the first to arrive. "Looks mighty pretty in here!"

Pinkie Pie was jumping up and down with excitement. "I know! I know!"

"I brought us a jug of cider and some apple muffins," said Applejack. "We had them left over when we finished up at the newspaper."

"That's perfect!" Pinkie Pie skipped

downstairs to answer the door. Fluttershy and Rarity were there.

"Hello!"

"Hello!"

"Hello!" Rarity had brought her keytar so the girls could jam together later on in the night, as well as a case of different-colored nail polishes.

"I want my toes to be pink!" exclaimed Pinkie Pie, and all the girls laughed together.

The girls loved their pillows. How did Pinkie Pie do it? She always had a special surprise waiting for her friends when they came over. It was so much fun to have a sleepover at her house.

When Sunset Shimmer arrived, she was thrilled with the pillow Pinkie Pie had made for her—until she saw the designs on the other girls'. They each had something that made them special. But what made her special other than her name? She didn't know. While the other girls painted one another's toes and fingers, she took her journal from her overnight bag to see if she'd heard anything from Twilight Sparkle. Nothing. She sighed.

"What color do you want to paint your toes?" asked Pinkie Pie.

"I want to paint my toes pink like you," Sunset Shimmer answered, and then immediately regretted her answer. Was she just copying? Wasn't there anything original about her at all?

But Pinkie Pie took it as a compliment. "Pink's always perfect!"

"You have such style, Sunset Shimmer," said Rarity.

Rainbow Dash arrived at the same time as the pizzas and brought the boxes up to the girls. But she wasn't hungry. She threw herself down on Pinkie Pie's bed in a huff.

"What's the matter?" asked Fluttershy, sitting beside her.

The other girls crowded around, concerned.

"It's our team uniforms," said Rainbow Dash. "It shouldn't matter, but they are old and faded. We're going to look so scrappy on the field compared to the other teams in the championship. We have to win this year to boost morale. Everyone is getting nervous about next year's Friendship Games."

"Why don't you buy new ones?" Sunset

Shimmer asked without looking up from painting her toes.

"We can't afford that right now," sighed Rainbow Dash.

The other girls nodded in agreement.

"It's not what you wear—it's how you play," Applejack said reassuringly.

"And our team practices so hard." Fluttershy touched her friend's hand.

"Uniforms don't matter that much," said Rarity, but tears welled up in her eyes. She hated to think of her friends having to look anything but their best.

"It's about morale," explained Rainbow Dash. "Sometimes it just gives the team that extra edge."

"Why don't we do some kind of fundraiser?" Sunset Shimmer screwed the top back on the nail polish and realized that all the girls were staring at her, their eyes wide. "We could do a bake sale or a car wash or a show and charge for tickets. It wouldn't be that hard." She took out her notebook. "If we take the number of kids in the school and multiply that by a reasonable ticket price and add in a little extra from a bake sale, subtracting, of course, what decorations would cost…"

The girls watched with amazement as she scribbled a line of numbers across the page.

"You're right!" Rarity clapped her hands.

"That's a brilliant idea, Sunset Shimmer! You are so smart!" exclaimed Rainbow Dash.

"Wow!" A huge smile lit up Fluttershy's face.

"Yes! Yes! Yes!" squealed Pinkie Pie. "A fund-raiser! We can make posters and flyers and tickets and invite everyone we know and it will be a huge success and this year we'll win the championship for sure!"

"Now, how come I didn't think of that?" asked Rainbow Dash.

Sunset Shimmer was thoughtful. "But we are going to have to decide exactly what kind of fund-raiser we want to do." She paused for a moment, her mind racing with possibilities. What was the best option? The girls were leaning in expectantly.

"I've got it!" she said at last. "A fashion show. And not just any kind of fashion show, but a way to show off designs for the new uniforms."

Rarity's eyes lit up. "I can create sample designs for new uniforms to show everyone...."

"And the kids on the teams can model

them! They'll love that." Rainbow Dash was very pleased.

"And we can have a bake sale, too!" Applejack rubbed her hands together as she thought about cooking up a mess of apple cider donuts with Granny Smith.

Fluttershy cleared her throat. "I have an idea," she chimed in softly. "What if we have a pet parade with animal fashions?"

"That's an adorable idea," said Rarity.

"Love it!" exclaimed Rainbow Dash.

"Totally cute," agreed Pinkie Pie. "And I'll be in charge of decorating."

All the girls burst out laughing. Of course Pinkie Pie would decorate, and it would be the best fund-raiser ever.

Fluttershy turned to Sunset Shimmer. "What do you want to do to help out?" she asked.

Sunset Shimmer looked taken aback. What was her special talent? "I don't know," she said.

"She had the idea, didn't she?" Apple-jack pointed out.

"Of course she did! She's full of them!" said Pinkie Pie, giving her a hug. "And you can help us all with getting the fashion show ready, isn't that right?"

"Absolutely," said Sunset Shimmer. "And I'll come up with something special that I can do. I don't know what. Yet. But something. Maybe we could write a new song for the Sonic Rainbooms to play. That might draw in even more people."

Rainbow Dash laughed. "Another great idea! You are amazing."

But Sunset Shimmer didn't feel amazing. She felt a little lost. She wanted some special way to contribute to the fashion show. What could she do? She didn't have any special talents like the other girls.

"It's time to practice, then," said Rarity. "Let me just tune up my keytar."

While the girls got ready to play, Sunset Shimmer slipped out of the room. She felt frustrated. All she had ever been interested in was magic. Pinkie Pie was an enthusiastic decorator, and Rarity was a skilled designer. Rainbow Dash was athletic, Applejack was an expert cook, and Fluttershy was gifted with animals. But all Sunset Shimmer could do was tag along. If only she could find some special way to stand out among her friends.

She glanced in her journal one last time—and there it was, an answer from Twilight Sparkle.

Dear Sunset Shimmer, wrote Twilight Sparkle. *You have always been such a good student, and now you have this wonderful opportunity to explore the Magic of Friendship. I know it doesn't always look that way, but it is the most powerful magic of all. I can't wait to hear what you find out and learn. Please let me know and say hi to everyone. I miss you all! Your friend, Twilight Sparkle.*

Rainbow Dash's guitar twanged from the other room, and Rarity began singing scales. Pinkie Pie tapped at her drum set, and Fluttershy's tambourine jangled. Each girl brought her own special sound to the music—and to the magic.

The girls were singing together now, and Sunset Shimmer peeked into the room. She already knew what she was going to see. The Sonic Rainbooms were ponying up. Ordinary girls were ponying up. Their pretty manes shook. Their ears twitched. Their pony tails swung from side to side. They were dancing and prancing and singing.

Every time she saw it, Sunset Shimmer was amazed. But how did it happen? What made it work?

Could it be that each girl's special talent also contributed to the magic in some way? Maybe what made Rainbow Dash such a star on the soccer field was also magic. Maybe Fluttershy's ability to communicate with animals was a kind of enchantment. Maybe it was time for Sunset Shimmer to leave her books behind and start investigating magic up close. Wasn't that what Twilight Sparkle had meant? In chemistry class, they didn't just learn formulas; they did experiments, too. That was it! While the girls worked on the fashion show, she was going to unlock the secrets of ponying up. That was her mission. That was what made her special. She was going to be a magic investigator. She imagined making a huge discovery that made the magic even better—and she would unveil it at the fashion show. She smiled and went back into the room to join the band. This was going to be so much fun!

Getting the Green Light

★ ★ ★

Sunset Shimmer volunteered to arrange all the details of the fashion show with Principal Celestia. When her classes were over the next day, Sunset went right to her office.

"It is a wonderful idea, and your music brings so much joy to the school," Principal Celestia agreed. "I'm just not sure if we can

add anything to the schedule at this late a date." She was clicking through different screens on her computer. "I'm sure we could make it happen for next year."

"But the championship is *this* year," said Sunset Shimmer, determined. "We need new uniforms as soon as possible. It will improve morale and maybe give us the extra edge to win!" Sunset Shimmer had planned her argument in advance. She was quite convincing.

"I realize that," said Principal Celestia. Her brow was furrowed as she continued to study the school schedule. "The only opening we have is next Friday, but that doesn't seem like enough time."

"Principal Celestia, we've put on proms in a day and concerts in a night, and you

know how responsible I am as a student. Right?"

Principal Celestia smiled. "That's true. You promise me that you can pull this off?"

"I promise!"

Sunset Shimmer practically skipped down the hall toward the doors that led to the athletic fields. She wanted to find Rainbow Dash and give her the good news.

Rainbow Dash was practicing with her teammates, bouncing the ball off her head, racing back and forth across the field, and kicking it straight through the posts. "Score!" she yelled, jumping up and down. When she came over to the sidelines to get a drink, Sunset Shimmer told her that they had a week to get ready for the fashion show.

"I told everyone on the team and they like the idea of new uniforms, but do you think we can do it that fast?" asked Rainbow Dash, concerned.

"No problem at all," said Sunset Shimmer confidently. "I've get everything under control and organized."

"I don't doubt that," said Rainbow Dash.

"But I do have one thing I would like to try with you. I'm doing a little research into magic."

"Yeah?"

Sunset Shimmer pulled out an elaborate wristband from her backpack. "Last night I designed a special device to measure your athletic ability—heartbeats per minute, steps taken, reaction times, everything." She handed it to Rainbow Dash, who slipped it on.

"Cool!" said Rainbow Dash, looking at the device already blinking on her wrist.

"See? You've taken three breaths, had two heartbeats, and your blood pressure hasn't changed. Impressive."

"I just have to wear it?" Rainbow Dash couldn't take her eyes off all the different numbers.

"That's all. I'll do the rest," said Sunset Shimmer. "I'm the magic investigator."

Rainbow Dash's teammates were calling for her. The practice game was about to continue.

"What else can we do with the magic?" asked Rainbow Dash, suddenly imagining goalies diverting balls with a word or being able to run as fast as a pony down the field.

Sunset Shimmer grinned as if she knew what Rainbow Dash was thinking. "Who knows? This fashion show is just the beginning! Now go!"

Rainbow Dash began dribbling the ball, but she kept checking her wrist. Every time she did, one of her classmates stole the ball from her. "It says I kick the ball with my foot every second and a half!" she called to Sunset Shimmer, who was watching from the sidelines. "Is that good or bad?"

"We don't know yet!" said Sunset Shimmer. "Just play! I'll keep track of everything on my monitor at home and interpret the data so we can figure out how to maximize your magic performance." She waved goodbye and went to find the other girls so she could tell them about the fashion show— and do a little high-tech research on their magic abilities, too.

Rainbow Dash could not focus on the

game. Each time she tapped the ball with her foot, the wristband buzzed. She got all turned around and began dribbling in the wrong direction. She caught the ball in her hands by accident, and she even kicked the ball right out of bounds into the woods. The coach was blowing her whistle and yelling, but Rainbow Dash didn't even notice. "Hey," she said happily. "That number that was one hundred twenty-six has gone up to one hundred thirty-eight! I think my footwork is getting better." The ball flew past her.

"How did you miss that?" yelled her teammate. "We've got the championship coming up! We can't waste a practice."

"What's the matter with you?" cried another girl in frustration.

But Rainbow Dash barely noticed the shouting. She couldn't take her eyes off the blinking lights. Even when she went into the locker room, she was paying attention to the number of steps she was taking and how much energy she was exerting. What she didn't notice was her teammates in a huddle, grumbling about the fashion show. What she didn't realize was that they didn't want anything to do with it. New uniforms might be nice—but not if getting them was going to mess with the talent of their star player.

CHAPTER

5

Made in the Shade

✴ ✴ ✴

Rarity was already hard at work on designs for the new uniforms in the art room. She had a paintbrush stuck in her hair, holding it up and keeping it out of her eyes, and she was drawing sketches for new uniforms on large sheets of white paper. Scattered on the table in front of her were swatches of fabric, clippings from magazines, pots of paint, markers, spools of thread, colored pencils, and a laptop.

Sunset Shimmer looked over her shoulder. "These color combinations are wonderful. I'm so glad we got the go-ahead from Principal Celestia. Do you think you can get a few samples ready in a week?"

"Darling, there is nothing I love better than fussing with fashion, although I will admit that a week is fast. But I can do it, and I'm grateful to you for giving me the opportunity!"

"Thank you," said Sunset Shimmer, pleased. "I was wondering if while you worked, I could take some photos of your designs. I'm doing a little research into the magic of the Sonic Rainbooms, and one of my theories is that it has something to do with color."

Rarity's eyes widened. "That's the smartest thing I've ever heard you say. Color is magical, and most people don't realize how the right blends and combinations can transform a look."

"Exactly! It may even have something to do with ponying up. You keep working, and I'm just going to click some photos with this special app I've developed to highlight hues outside the ordinary rainbow spectrum. I want to see if there is something going on that we don't usually notice."

Rarity waved her hand. "Click away! Don't mind me!"

Sunset Shimmer took a slew of photos from all different angles—of the fabric, of the designs, and of Rarity hard at work. Her hypothesis was that she would capture some kind of special light or aura that revealed the secrets of the magic. But she would need a lot of photos to verify her results. How would she find the time to review them all?

That's when it hit her. Crowdsourcing! She could upload the photos to the Sonic Rainbooms website and invite their fans to look for signs of magic. What a brilliant idea. With one final click, she uploaded all the photos to the band's page.

"Thanks, Rarity, I think I've got enough photos for some potentially interesting results. Let me know if you need any help with anything."

"I will, Sunset," said Rarity without looking up from her work.

Out in the hall, Sunset Shimmer realized what fun she was having. She liked being a magic investigator—and it gave her an opportunity to be with her friends after school. Now she had her own hobby, just like them. And to top it off, she was sure to make some potentially important breakthroughs in the study of magic. Maybe one day she'd even win a prize for her discoveries!

Sunset Shimmer was so excited that she pulled out her journal and dashed off a quick note to Twilight Sparkle.

Dear Twilight Sparkle, she wrote. *You were right! I am so grateful that you reminded me that magic is everywhere because at last I am seeing what's possible at Canterlot High. You won't believe what I'm going to discover and make happen here. More later! I've got so much to do! We're all putting on a fashion show together. Wish you were here!*

A moment later, a pink heart magically appeared underneath her note. From Twilight Sparkle. Sunset Shimmer pranced down the hall to the cafeteria. She was definitely on the right track!

Back in the art room, Rarity's phone started buzzing with texts. At first, she ignored them because she had so much to do, but then she became worried that something was the matter with one of her friends—it turned out something was the matter with her!

"Rarity, are you sick? You're so green in that photo!"

"Yikes! We're not going to look like that when we model the uniforms, are we?"

"Girl, what has happened to your style?"

"Are you okay?"

What were they talking about? She

dashed off a quick text to Pinkie Pie. *"Everyone is talking about some photo of me. Do you know what's going on?"*

"No idea! Why would you put such an ugly photo of yourself up on our website?"

Rarity gulped, remembering Sunset Shimmer's magic research. Could it be? She opened her laptop and went to the Sonic Rainbooms' page. And there she was, her eyes squinting, her hair all mussed and tangled, her tongue sticking out of her mouth a little bit while she drew, and strange mossy green speckles covering her nose and cheeks like pimples. She looked terrible. Just terrible. Was this what she really looked like? How could she call herself a fashionista and look like that?

Her phone was buzzing with more messages. But she couldn't look at them. She slumped in her chair. How would she ever live this down? She couldn't work any more on the designs for the team uniforms today. She had to do some serious damage control if anyone was going to trust her to tell them what to wear ever again.

CHAPTER

6

A Tempest in the Kitchen

★ ★ ★

"Magic?" Applejack wasn't so sure she believed Sunset Shimmer. "What are you investigating magic for, anyway? We've got enough magic going on when we play music."

The girls were standing in the middle of the cafeteria kitchen, where Applejack was cooking up a mess of donuts. She'd organized her mixing bowls and baking sheets and cooking racks. She'd bought eggs, sugar, flour, salt, seasonings, milk, and lots of apples. There was nothing Applejack liked better than baking. Besides, she'd finish it all up this afternoon and still have plenty of time to work on that week's edition of the school paper.

"I'm experimenting with magic the way you do with cooking," explained Sunset Shimmer.

"I always follow a recipe," said Applejack.

"But we don't really know the recipe yet," said Sunset Shimmer. "Every time you whip up a batch of donuts, people ask what the secret ingredient is, don't they?"

"And I always tell them there isn't one," said Applejack. "Because there isn't."

"That's where you're wrong!" Sunset Shimmer was excited.

"I am?" Applejack scratched her head, confused.

"There must be. Only it's magic flowing out of you, possibly the very same ingredient that sets off the reaction that results in everyone ponying up when we play our music. That's my theory, anyway. I've been reading a lot about alchemy in preparation for this."

"If you say so," said Applejack, unconvinced. "What do I do? I have a schedule I've got to keep to if I'm going to get all these goodies ready for the bake sale."

"You don't have to do anything," said Sunset Shimmer. "I'm just going to be setting up a few monitoring devices and doing some field research, taking notes, asking questions, that kind of thing."

Sunset Shimmer set up a heat monitor near the oven and put a thermometer with wires sticking out of it into the mixing bowl.

"Whoa!" said Applejack, just as she was about to pour in a few cups of flour. "What's that?"

"Just measuring temperature fluctuations. Don't mind me."

Every time Applejack reached for an ingredient, however, it seemed like Sunset Shimmer was already there—running some kind of scanner over the salt or the milk or the butter. "You finding anything interesting?"

"Not yet," said Sunset Shimmer. "But you have to be patient and observant when you are a magic investigator."

"Same with cooking," said Applejack.

Applejack tossed eggshells into the trash, and Sunset Shimmer retrieved them, documenting the size and shape of each crack. Applejack picked up the electric mixer, and Sunset Shimmer attached an electrode to it. Applejack went to take a look at her recipe book and couldn't find it anywhere. Sunset Shimmer was reading it and had lost her page.

"Recipes are really like spells, aren't they?" she observed.

"Maybe," said Applejack. "But I need to know how many spoonfuls of baking powder I'm supposed to put in these donuts."

"Oh, I'm sorry," said Sunset Shimmer, handing her the book. "This is all so fascinating."

"This is all so confusing," said Applejack,

trying to remember what she was supposed to do next. "What's all this commotion got to do with how we pony up, anyway?"

"Ah!" said Sunset Shimmer, thrilled to be asked a question. "If we can isolate the different variables of enchantment and tweak them, it's very possible that we will be able to maximize our musical magic."

"Could you put that into plain English, please?"

"I'm trying to figure out how to make our magic!"

"Oh?" Applejack wasn't watching what she was doing and accidentally poured all the milk out of the carton—and onto the floor. "Shoot!"

"Here. I'll clean that up for you," said Sunset Shimmer. She went to grab the mop and pulled on one of the wires attached to the mixer, which went skittering across the counter, spilling batter everywhere. "Oops."

"Now I've got one big barnyard of a mess to clean up!"

As Sunset Shimmer began mopping, smoke started billowing from the oven and an acrid smell filled the air. "My first batch!" shouted Applejack, rushing toward the stove with pot holders. But it was too late. The treats were scorched.

Sunset Shimmer felt terrible. "I think the heat monitor may have increased the temperature. Sometimes that happens."

"Well," said Applejack, "at least you didn't turn into a she-devil or sow disharmony or anything like that."

Sunset Shimmer gulped, remembering

the mistakes of her past. The girls were so nice and accepting, it was easy for her to forget that once she had nearly destroyed the whole school. But she would never do anything like that again. That was what was important about her magic investigations— if she understood magic better, she could make sure it was always used for good.

"What's going on in here?" asked Granny Smith, coming into the kitchen. "Looks like you girls are cookin' up trouble! What a mess!" She picked up another broom and began sweeping all the ingredients for the fashion show bake sale into a pile for the trash.

Applejack handed Sunset Shimmer a dishrag. "It's not very magical, but it gets the job done."

Sunset Shimmer scrubbed until the kitchen was spotless. But the whole time she was wondering how she could figure out the Sonic Rainbooms' special magic. There had to be a secret ingredient—but what could it be?

Blueprint for Disaster

* * *

That night, just before she was about to go to sleep, Sunset Shimmer noticed her journal was glowing. A message from Twilight Sparkle.

Remember, wrote the Princess of Friendship. *Magic is sometimes in the places we least expect.*

Had Sunset somehow been wrong about the Sonic Rainbooms and their hidden abilities? Or was she not thinking about magic in the right way? What did Twilight Sparkle mean? *Magic is sometimes in the places we least expect.* Where did she least expect to find magic? What was the secret ingredient? She'd been reviewing the data from Rainbow Dash's wrist monitor, but it still hadn't shown anything special—nor did the color-change photos of Rarity that she had studied. Still, she was determined to solve this problem. She liked hard problems. Where wasn't she looking? It hit her!

Fluttershy. Of course.

The shyest, sweetest member of the Sonic Rainbooms. She didn't perform fancy guitar riffs or sing foot-stomping solos, but maybe, just maybe...could it be that as she quietly tapped her tambourine on the side of the stage, she was generating the powerful magic? That must be it! Why hadn't she thought of it herself?

She pulled out her phone and sent a quick text. *"Hey, Fluttershy! Can I come help you at the animal shelter tomorrow?"*

"Yes!" came the immediate answer. *"Can't wait."*

Sunset Shimmer thought about Fluttershy. It made sense, really, that with her love of animals she would have the most access to Equestrian magic. She just didn't know she was a powerful magician. But with Sunset Shimmer's expert guidance, she might be able to release her true powers. Then Fluttershy would admire her as a magic investigator—and be grateful to have her as a friend.

Fluttershy was cleaning out the hamster cages when Sunset Shimmer arrived at the shelter the next day. She had a laptop, a camera, and a whole series of notebooks.

"Be sure to shut the door carefully behind you," said Fluttershy. "We don't want any escapees," she told her friend. "I'll just finish this up, and you can cuddle some of the new kittens that just arrived. They need lots of reassurance. Would that be all right?"

"Sure!" agreed Sunset Shimmer as Fluttershy placed three purring balls of fluff in her lap. Magic could wait when there were kittens to pet.

"Can I ask you a question?" Fluttershy

spread new cedar chips on the floor of the hamster cage.

"Anything," said Sunset Shimmer.

"What do you miss most about Equestria?"

"What?" Sunset Shimmer was stunned. No one ever really asked her about her old life.

"Do you miss your pony friends there?"

"My friends?" Sunset Shimmer hadn't really *had* friends there. Mostly she'd been focused on figuring out the secrets to Celestia's magic so she could be the supreme ruler of the pony world. "Not really," she said. "I was different then."

Fluttershy nodded. "I just know that when my rescues come in, it can take a while for them to get used to being here."

Sunset Shimmer paused. "It's been a

learning experience, but I think I'm doing okay for a rescue."

"Of course you are," said Fluttershy sweetly. "I love your fashion show idea. I've made replicas of Rarity's uniforms for the animals to wear in their parade. It's going to be so cute. You want to see how they model them?"

"Absolutely!"

Fluttershy took out a whistle, which made no sound when she blew into it. Still, the kittens hopped out of Sunset Shimmer's lap. The puppies bounded over, and even the hamsters got in a line.

"How did you get them to do that?" asked Sunset Shimmer, amazed.

"Animals can hear sounds at frequencies that we can't detect, so I use special whistles and clicks to communicate with them."

"Twilight Sparkle was right!" exclaimed Sunset Shimmer. "You are magic."

Fluttershy blushed. "No, just patient."

Sunset Shimmer paced as she came up with a new experiment. "It's just possible that you are generating a series of magical notes that—if we could detect and work into our song—would increase the magical force field."

"Why would we want to do that?"

"Magic is a force for good in the world. Think if the Sirens showed up again. We'd want to know how to use our full powers, right?"

"That makes sense," said Fluttershy.

"Would you mind if I hooked that whistle up to an amp when we are practicing this afternoon?"

"I don't think there would be a problem with that."

"I think it's going to be very exciting," said Sunset Shimmer breathlessly. "I can't wait to try it. Maybe we could go over to the auditorium right now. This is going to be the experiment that breaks everything wide open. People don't realize that magic investigators sometimes have to make a lot of mistakes before they have a breakthrough."

"Okay," said Fluttershy. "Right now?"

"Hurry!" said Sunset Shimmer. "I want to try this out as soon as possible."

Fluttershy poured some food into the animals' bowls and turned out the lights. The two girls hurried out of the shelter together. It was only when they were partway to school that Sunset Shimmer realized she'd left her laptop and phone behind. She could be such an absentminded scientist, but she needed to keep track of her ongoing investigations.

"I'll go back and get them for you," said Fluttershy.

"No, you go on ahead and set up the instruments. I need some time to think about the adjustments for this experiment."

Lost in thoughts of wattage and electricity, she barely noticed the animals weaving in and out between her legs at the shelter. She gathered up her things and hurried back out the door—forgetting to shut it behind her when she left.

CHAPTER

8

Sunset Shimmer's True Colors?

★ ★ ★

Pinkie Pie was in the auditorium, covered in paint and glitter. She was working on a backdrop for the fashion show. "Grab a brush," she said when Fluttershy arrived. "I'm filling it with rainbows and flowers and ponies and balloons and everything we love!"

Fluttershy skipped over to join her, but Sunset Shimmer, just behind her, stopped. "Actually, Pinkie Pie, we are going to try a magic experiment, if you would like to lend a hand."

"What kind of magic experiment?"

"Sunset Shimmer is trying to find out why we pony up," explained Fluttershy.

"Because it's fun?" said Pinkie Pie.

"It's not just about fun," said Sunset Shimmer. "There is a mechanism to the magic that I am trying to unlock and reveal so that, if we need to, we can adjust the control settings and create an enhanced pony-up experience."

Pinkie Pie's eyes went wide. "Will we still have fun if we do all that?"

Sunset Shimmer realized she was not yet ready to explain magic equations to Pinkie

Pie. "Would you play some drums for us during the experiment?" she asked.

"Sure!" said Pinkie Pie. "It's always fun to play the drums."

While the girls got the bands' instruments arranged, Sunset Shimmer checked her laptop. She noted that Rainbow Dash's blood pressure was steadily increasing. Something seemed to be happening to her, although it was hard to tell exactly what. She switched over to the website for an update on the color-detection process, but the whole site was down for some reason. She'd have to look into that later.

"We're ready to play music and sing," said Fluttershy. "For the experiment."

"Perfect," said Sunset Shimmer. "Let me just hook up that whistle of yours to an amp—and my computer monitor. You know, it's like chemistry—you have all the right ingredients, but then it takes a spark to trigger the reaction."

"If it's like chemistry, I might not be very good at it," Pinkie Pie said.

"Shall we just start jamming and see what happens?" suggested Fluttershy.

"Can you blow the whistle and play your tambourine at the same time?" asked Sunset Shimmer.

"Easy," said Fluttershy.

Pinkie Pie picked up her drumsticks. "One...two..." The girls began singing together.

"Hey, hey, everybody,
We've got something to say.
We may seem as different
As the night is from day.

But you look a little deeper,
And you will see
That I'm just like you
And you're just like me.
Yeah!"

Pinkie Pie's hair was flying and turning into a mane as she drummed. Fluttershy was lifting her knees and beginning to prance, and Sunset Shimmer was studying them, trying to see if she could detect a word, an action, or a sound that made the magic happen. The amp didn't seem to be doing anything.

Sunset Shimmer was feeling more and more frustrated. The magic happened, but she couldn't figure it out. Maybe she was a failure as a magic investigator—but there was nothing else she was any good at. Everyone was doing something special for the fashion show, and she wanted to do something special, too. It would be terrible if she had nothing to show for her efforts. She adjusted the controls on the amp.

Just then, Rainbow Dash burst into the auditorium. "We've got to cancel the fashion show. The team wants new uniforms— but everyone is mad at me, and I can't figure out why because I'm burning more calories than ever." Rainbow Dash was checking her wristband again, and without looking, she knocked a bottle of glitter onto the floor.

"Oops!" said Pinkie Pie, rushing over to pick it up.

Rarity arrived a moment later. She had curled her hair and was wearing an entirely new outfit with matching accessories. "I'm sorry I'm behind on the uniform designs," she apologized. "But I have been having to focus on my own style. You would not believe the horrible things people were saying about my hair online."

Sunset Shimmer waved her hand at them, trying to get everyone to be quiet. "Something is coming through on the monitor. Something is happening! Eureka! I think I may have found the source of the magic. It's getting closer and closer and closer!"

The girls all crowded around Sunset Shimmer's laptop.

"If you find the source of the magic," whispered Rainbow Dash, "can you make my teammates less angry at me?"

"Will it convince people I've got a fashion sense again?"

"Will it make me another batch of

donuts?" Applejack had arrived, covered in flour. She was exhausted from having to spend another afternoon in the kitchen.

"Shhh!" said Sunset Shimmer. "I'm trying to figure out this reading...."

Everyone was very quiet. They didn't dare breathe. The only sound was a steady beep coming from the laptop. A green line was going up and up and up.

"Meow?" said a tiny voice.

The girls whirled around. Coming into the auditorium was a tiny kitten, looking scared and frightened.

"What are you doing here?" said Fluttershy. "How did you ever get out?" She ran over and picked up the kitten.

Sunset Shimmer looked at the kitten and, with a terrible feeling in her stomach, realized that she had forgotten to shut the shelter door. Then she'd amped the pet whistle, calling all the animals to Fluttershy. Now they were probably all on the loose thanks to her.

As if to confirm her worst suspicions, Principal Celestia appeared. She did not look happy. "What is going on in this school? The cafeteria kitchen is in shambles, and the art room is littered with fabric. I've got athletes coming into my office telling me there is no way they want to do a fashion show, and I just got a call from the animal shelter that all the animals have somehow escaped."

"My rescues!" gasped Fluttershy.

Principal Celestia held up her hand. "In a minute, Fluttershy, we'll organize the whole school to give you a hand finding them, but right now, I want to know if this is your idea of a fashion show. Sunset Shimmer, I thought you told me you were up to this challenge. I expected more leadership from you."

Sunset Shimmer looked down at her feet, disappointed in herself. But she wasn't a quitter. "Principal Celestia, I want to make this up to the whole school. I made a promise, and I'm going to keep it. We'll have everything cleaned up by this afternoon, and the fashion show will be ready to go by tomorrow night."

"You sure?"

"I'm sure," said Sunset Shimmer.

"That's what I want to hear," said Principal Celestia. "Now, about those animals…"

"Give me one minute and we'll all be right there."

Principal Celestia gave Sunset Shimmer one last stern look before leaving, but Sunset Shimmer knew the other girls were looking at her—and they were upset with her, too. She had thought she had a magic problem to solve. But she didn't. She had a friendship problem, and it was all her own fault.

Sunset Shimmer had been so focused on investigating the elements of magic that she'd overlooked the most important thing of all—friendship. You couldn't measure it, photograph it, amp it, or dissect it, but it was real and it's what really made everything happen. That was the secret ingredient. Friendship.

She took a big breath. "I've made a lot of mistakes over the past two days." She braced herself for everyone's anger. She was sure they were going to yell at her or, even worse, storm out and never speak to her again. "I'm sorry I've made so many problems for everyone."

"But no one's better at solving problems than you!" said Pinkie Pie.

All the girls laughed. It was true.

"You think you can persuade my teammates to model in the fashion show?" asked Rainbow Dash.

"Can you repair my style status?" asked Rarity.

"Can you do some real cooking?"

"Can you blow up some balloons?"

"I can do it all," said Sunset Shimmer, determined to be a good friend. "But the first thing we all need to do is rescue Fluttershy's animals. Right, Fluttershy?"

She handed Fluttershy her pet whistle—
and removed the amp.

"Right!" said her friend.

"All right, then," said Sunset Shimmer.
"Let's go."

CHAPTER

9

After the Storm

$$\star\ \star\ \star$$

It was the hardest letter Sunset Shimmer had ever written to Twilight Sparkle.

Dear Twilight Sparkle, she wrote. *I may be getting good grades in school, but I think I'm failing in friendship. I just wish there was something that made me special, like the other girls have, but the only thing I'm good at is making a mess of everything.*

She had not even put down her pen when the journal began to glow. Twilight Sparkle had written her back instantaneously.

Dear Sunset Shimmer, wrote Twilight Sparkle. *What happened? Can you tell me everything?*

Tears fell from Sunset Shimmer's cheeks, blotching the ink on the page as it all poured out of her. *All the other girls have something that makes them special. They are athletic and creative and artistic and good with animals, and I'm not really good at anything. Except I used to be good at magic and I thought maybe I could somehow be Canterlot High's very own magic investigator. I tried to make magic happen—and instead all I did was ruin everything. Applejack's donuts are burnt, and*

Fluttershy's animals are missing, and it's all my fault.

She wouldn't be surprised if she didn't hear back from Twilight Sparkle. How many times could the princess forgive her?

But within an instant, the journal was glowing again.

Maybe you've been investigating the wrong thing at Canterlot High. You've already learned a lot about magic. Maybe now is the time to learn something else. Do you think you can really be a student again? Are you ready to learn? What can each of your friends teach you? That's the important question.

Sunset Shimmer was still a little bit confused. *The girls can teach me about magic?* she wrote back to Twilight Sparkle. *How?*

Dear Sunset Shimmer, wrote Twilight Sparkle. *The Magic of Friendship has special charms, and each of your friends is an expert at one of them. Together they are unstoppable. But it's best if you find that out for yourself. You were a great student of magic in Equestria. I think you can be a great student of friendship. Are you ready?*

Sunset Shimmer felt like her whole world had wibbled and wobbled. She didn't know anything. *Where do I start?* she wrote.

Jump in and lend a hand. That's what you did when the Sirens were threatening the school. Seems like there's an emergency at the animal shelter. And I think it's a good idea if you check in with me whenever you want. Consider me your friendship tutor. Is that okay?

Yes! wrote back Sunset Shimmer. *But now I have to go round up some kittens and puppies!*

CHAPTER

10

♥ut of the Blue

★ ★ ★

Kids were spread out all over town. They were searching the Sweet Shoppe and the athletic fields. They were leaving trails of catnip back to the shelter. "Here, kitty, kitty, puppy, puppy," they were calling. Some were blowing whistles, and others were making high-pitched clucking noises. But none of it seemed to be working. No one had found the missing animals.

Sunset Shimmer had no idea where to start. She felt helpless. Probably the best thing to do, she decided, was to find Fluttershy and ask for directions. If anyone knew how to rescue pets, it was her.

She ran up and down the streets until she saw Fluttershy standing by herself in a vacant lot. It was not that far from the shelter. Fluttershy was standing very still as if she were frozen. And she wasn't making a sound.

"Hey, Fluttershy!" Sunset Shimmer called out.

But Fluttershy didn't move. She held her finger to her lips and motioned for Sunset Shimmer to come close.

"What are you doing?" whispered Sunset Shimmer when she was right beside her.

"Listening," Fluttershy said softly. "They are lost and lonely, and they want to be found. That's what you need to know. If we are very, very quiet and listen, I'm sure we'll find them not far from here."

"That's all we have to do?"

"That's it." Fluttershy smiled. "Listen."

"Why don't you use your whistle?"

"Outside and far away from me, it would only confuse them. That's just for tricks, not finding their way home."

"Okay, then I'll go looking...and listening."

As quietly as she could, Sunset Shimmer began walking up the street. She stopped by trees and garbage cans. She tried to make very little noise. She heard birds singing and cars honking and the kids calling in the distance. But she didn't hear the kittens or the puppies. Where could they be? It was her fault that they had gotten lost. She had forgotten to shut the door. If only she could make it up to everyone.

She paused. Her heart was beating very loudly. She tried to think where she would go if she were a lost kitten. *Not far* was her first thought. Not far at all. It must seem very scary out in the world to those little ones. She started walking back toward the shelter. And that's when she heard a little voice crying out. "Meow, meow, meow," it squeaked. "Yip, yip, yip," cried someone else from a scraggly bush by the sidewalk.

Gently, carefully, so as not to frighten them, she pulled up a branch. Huddled together in the dirt were the kittens and puppies. *Oh,* thought Sunset Shimmer, *you poor, scared things.*

"Come here, sweethearts," she called to them, bending down. But they didn't really know her, and they scooted farther into the bush as she tried to reach for them. "I'm getting Fluttershy," she told them.

She raced back to the vacant lot and told Fluttershy that she'd found the animals.

"Oh, thank you!" said Fluttershy. "I knew you would!"

When they got to the bush, they could hear the kittens and puppies meowing softly. "How are we going to get them out?" asked Sunset Shimmer.

Fluttershy laughed. "Now, this really is magic that I'm going to show you!" She took a can of pet food out of her pocket and popped the lid. Instantly, she was surrounded by eager furry friends wrapping themselves around her ankles. Sunset Shimmer laughed, too, and together the girls picked up the kittens and puppies and carried them back to the shelter.

When everyone was settled safely back inside their cages with some warm milk and treats, Fluttershy sat herself down in front of them and began asking each animal simple questions. "How was it? Was it scary?" she asked. The kittens meowed and purred and hissed, and the puppies yipped and barked and howled almost as if they were talking to her. And Fluttershy nodded her head almost as if she understood what they were all saying. Maybe she did.

Watching her, Sunset Shimmer remembered Fluttershy asking *her* if she missed being in Equestria. The question had surprised Sunset Shimmer and made her a little sad because all she had wanted in the old days was to be the most powerful one of all. She didn't have any friends back in Equestria. But she did now, and she wanted to keep them.

That's when Sunset Shimmer finally realized what Fluttershy's special magic was. She was a good listener. She asked questions, and she genuinely wanted to hear the answers. That was the thing about Fluttershy—she didn't speak up very often, she wasn't showy, but it was often because she was listening and observing what was happening around her. She cared about how everyone was doing. If everybody was always talking and no one was listening to anyone else, how could you be friends?

Could Sunset Shimmer learn the magic of listening? She hoped so.

"Hey, Fluttershy," she said softly. "I just want to apologize for leaving the door open."

"It's not your fault," answered Fluttershy.

"It is," said Sunset Shimmer, "and I'm sorry. Are you angry with me?"

"I was a little," admitted Fluttershy, "but how can I be now that you found everyone?"

"Thank you so much. That means a lot to me. I was wondering if sometimes I could help you out here at the shelter. I'd like to learn to talk to the animals like you do."

"Would you?"

"I would," said Sunset Shimmer. And she meant it.

"That is the best thing I've heard in forever." Fluttershy was beaming.

Picking up the Pieces

★ ★ ★

Sunset Shimmer had a lot of repair work to do, and her next stop was the cafeteria kitchen. Applejack was busily mixing up batter while the aroma of donuts wafted through the air. Sunset Shimmer poked her head into the room. "Can I come in?" she asked.

Applejack startled. "Whoa! I just got this whole place cleaned up, and I might just get us some donuts for the bake sale—if you don't start experimenting with magic.... You can stay right there."

Sunset Shimmer hung her head in embarrassment. "Are you angry with me?" she asked.

"Angry?" Applejack snorted. "I am white-hot furious at the ruckus you've caused, but the last thing I need is another cupful of trouble."

Sunset Shimmer gulped. At least Applejack was honest. "I'm truly sorry," she apologized in a soft voice.

"You tellin' the truth?" asked Applejack warily. She seemed to have calmed down after having been given an opportunity to express her feelings.

"I can understand why you wouldn't believe me, but I really want to make it up to you. I'm willing to do whatever you want me to—cream butter, crack eggs, wash dishes, you name it."

"It's true I could use some help," said Applejack. "Can you follow directions, girl?"

Sunset Shimmer nodded. "Just tell me what to do. I'm all ears."

Sunset Shimmer mixed and stirred. She enjoyed carefully paring the apples so that the skin came off in one single peel. She loved putting the donuts into the fryer and watching them turn golden brown. It was just like magic, it really was.

"C'mon over here," said Applejack at last. "I need your help frosting these donuts."

"Really?"

"Course I do! Do I ever lie?"

In fact she didn't.

That was the thing about Applejack. She was always direct and honest about her feelings. Sometimes, it made her seem a little impolite, but in fact, it really meant that you always knew where you stood with her. There was no beating around the bush, and there was never any lying.

"How should I decorate them? What should they look like?"

"Hmmm," said Applejack. "I was just going to slap on the frosting. But it would be kind of fun to fancy them up, wouldn't it?"

Sunset Shimmer grinned. "It would."

Applejack scratched her head. "You got any ideas?"

"We could make them look like soccer balls for Rainbow Dash, or maybe we could do a Wondercolt theme—horseshoes and tails and stars and rainbows."

"Now that's a super idea!"

"It is?"

"Would I lie to you?"

Sunset Shimmer laughed. "You would not."

There was lots of giggling as the girls frosted the donuts. They added swirls and sprinkles. Sunset Shimmer discovered that she wasn't bad at decorating and was good at using the pastry bag to create pretty designs. When all the donuts were frosted, they looked beautiful—and delicious. There was still frosting left in the bowl, and Applejack swiped her spatula in it and frosted Sunset Shimmer's nose! Then Sunset Shimmer did the same to Applejack.

"Now we're decorated." The girls laughed.

They wiped their faces clean and licked the last of the frosting from their fingers.

"That didn't take any time at all!" said Sunset Shimmer, amazed.

"You are wrong about that," said Applejack, pointing at the clock. Hours had passed.

"But…," wondered Sunset Shimmer. "How could that be?"

"When you are doing something fun, time disappears," explained Applejack. "That's its own kind of magic."

"You are right," agreed Sunset Shimmer. "But you left one thing out. When you are doing something fun with a friend, that's the most magic of all."

After the girls had carefully stored the donuts, Applejack invited Sunset Shimmer over to her house.

"I wish I could come," said Sunset Shimmer. "But I need to see how Rarity's doing with her sewing."

"That's right," said Applejack, remembering. "Mind if I come along?"

"Absolutely not," said Sunset Shimmer in all honesty. "I just have to write a quick note to a friend first."

Sunset Shimmer took out her journal. *Dear Twilight Sparkle,* she wrote. *I think I am finally beginning to discover some of the magic you were talking about. And you know what? I think I've needed to learn about it for a long time. By the way, Twilight Sparkle, I've been wondering how you are doing? How is everything in Equestria?*

A moment later, a glowing friendship heart appeared under her note. Twilight Sparkle wrote, *Why, thank you for asking! There is a lot to share and I would love to tell you all about it. . . . More soon!*

CHAPTER

12

A golden opportunity

★ ★ ★

Walking through the halls with Apple-jack, Sunset Shimmer was amazed to see that Pinkie Pie had put up posters for the fashion show everywhere. COME SUPPORT OUR TEAMS! ANIMALS, MUSIC, AND FASHION! TICKETS AVAILABLE NOW!

Sunset Shimmer's heart skipped a beat.

She really hoped that the evening would still be a success.

When she and Applejack arrived at the art room, Rarity was studying three different designs—one of which transformed the athletes into ponies with tails. "I just can't choose," she said. "I've lost my flair for fashion."

"You could never lose that!" said Sunset Shimmer.

"Did you see me in those photos?" sighed Rarity.

"I didn't when I took them," said Sunset Shimmer. "I was only thinking about myself and my investigation and not about you and how you would feel. But I won't ever do that again."

"I like this uniform with the pony tails,"

said Applejack. "It's really cute. I'd wear that."

"You don't think it's too much?" asked Rarity, uncertain. "It's the one I like the most, too, but I'm worried everyone is going to hate it."

"Hey, I have an idea," said Sunset Shimmer.

Rarity and Applejack exchanged alarmed glances.

"It's not about magic," said Sunset Shimmer quickly. "It's about fashion. What if I created an app that let every kid on a team see what the uniform would actually look like on them while they are playing soccer or basketball or baseball? Would that help?"

"It might," said Applejack encouragingly.

Rarity wasn't so sure. "What if the kids

don't think the uniforms are original enough? I mean, I understand the need for everyone to have their own personal style in some way. That's what fashion's all about. You know, there's no reason athletes can't be fashionable on the field."

"But how can you do that?" asked Applejack. "You can't make a special costume for every player. Uniforms are supposed to be all the same."

"That's true," said Rarity. "Still, there ought to be a way for all the athletes to make the uniforms their own."

Sunset Shimmer was impressed by her friend's thoughtfulness. Style wasn't just about clothes and hair to her—it was about personal expression, about finding a way to be who you really are. That was a real gift Rarity had, to help people look and feel good about themselves. It made Sunset Shimmer feel even more terrible about having snapped such unflattering photos of her. What could she do to help? That was the only question.

Sunset Shimmer looked around the room for inspiration. Sticking out of Rarity's backpack was the special pillow Pinkie Pie had created for her friends at the sleepover. "That's it!" shouted Sunset Shimmer. "I've got an idea. Rarity, is it possible to create some kind of design element that would be special to each player? Maybe it's attachable?"

"Like with snaps?" asked Rarity.

Sunset Shimmer clapped her hands. "Exactly! We could create a variety of ways that kids could personalize their uniforms on the app and turn them into decals. Applejack could put an apple on hers, for instance."

"I'd like that!" said Applejack.

"See?" said Sunset Shimmer.

Rarity was nodding her head. "I like it, too. I really do. It lets everybody bring their own unique sense of style to the game. There's only one problem. How are we ever going to get that all ready by tomorrow?"

"She's right," said Applejack. "I've got homework to do."

Rarity sighed. "Me too."

"I don't have any," said Sunset Shimmer.

"Really?" Applejack was amazed.

"Would I lie to you?" Sunset Shimmer smiled. "Rarity, if you show me how to make decals, I can create a bunch of different ones tonight. Then kids can choose their own for the fashion show."

Rarity hugged Sunset Shimmer. "You are amazing. The best student in the whole school and the best friend ever."

"Oh." Sunset Shimmer blushed. "I am not the best friend. Not yet, anyway. I have a lot to learn about friendship. But luckily I have some good friends to show me the ropes."

Sunset Shimmer opened her laptop and began hitting the keys. She showed Rarity the app she was creating. "Could you model the first one and show everyone how to do it?"

Rarity laughed. "If you let me do my hair first and don't turn my nose green."

"Promise!" said Sunset Shimmer. "I am not posting any photos without your approval."

Applejack and Rarity watched with

amazement as Sunset Shimmer set up the app. She clicked buttons and dragged photos and opened windows like it was as easy as, well, magic. Finally, she looked up and smiled at her friends.

"It's ready. I've sent a link to each of your phones and we can go down to the fields together and start showing everyone how to use it. I don't think they'll be able to resist the new uniforms, or the fashion show, once they see how great they look."

"Me neither!" said Rarity, pleased.

And they couldn't.

Sunset Shimmer, Applejack, and Rarity went down to the soccer field and called all the players over. They started mixing and matching their faces and bodies into the uniform designs.

"Wow!"

"Awesome!"

"I look great!"

"And you can personalize them with your very own decals that Sunset Shimmer is going to make!" announced Rarity.

"How did you ever create such a cool app?" asked one of the teammates.

"It was easy," said Sunset Shimmer. "I just used all the data I had in my computer from Rainbow Dash's wrist monitor." She reached over to her friend and slipped the distracting device over her hand. "But we're done with that now. I realize it interfered with her playing, but it was so helpful for me." She winked at Rarity.

Rainbow Dash was blinking her eyes as if she were returning to the real world. "I'm going to miss knowing how many breaths I'm taking per minute."

"You know what?" said Sunset Shimmer. "I think you might actually play better not knowing that."

Everyone burst out laughing because she was absolutely right. Sometimes investigating something was a surefire way to ruin it, and Sunset Shimmer realized that maybe learning about friendship meant being a good friend and not experimenting with it.

CHAPTER

13

Tickled Pink

✦ ✦ ✦

Pinkie Pie had gone all out. She had decorated the cafeteria to advertise the fashion show. There were posters. There were balloons. There were streamers. There was even a TV monitor set up showing one of the Sonic Rainbooms' sell-out performances. Pinkie Pie herself was going from table to table selling tickets to the evening's big event.

Sunset Shimmer slid into a seat beside Rarity and handed her a big box of attachable decals she had made. She covered a yawn with her hand.

"How long did it take you to do all of this?" Rarity asked in amazement.

"Not as long as it took you to design all those uniforms," Sunset Shimmer answered.

"The kittens and puppies are ready for their parade!" Fluttershy announced as she sat down. "I can't wait for tonight. It's going to be wonderful."

"I even had some extra time to whip up a special batch of my famous cider," said Applejack. "How did we ever manage to get everything done?"

"Teamwork," said Rainbow Dash. "It's what does it every time."

Sunset Shimmer looked around the table at each of her friends. Each one of them was so different and so special. She was really lucky.

Pinkie Pie took a break from selling tickets and came over to sit with them. She looked upset.

"What's the matter, Pinkie Pie?" asked Sunset Shimmer, concerned.

"I don't really know," said Pinkie Pie. "I've tried to show everyone how fun the fashion show is going to be, but nobody is buying tickets. Nobody. Not even DJ Pon-3. Not even Flash. I can't imagine what's going on. Nothing else is scheduled for tonight. I don't even think there are any parties. Believe me, if there were, I would know."

"That's so strange," said Rainbow Dash.

"I never imagined people wouldn't come," said Applejack.

"The athletes told me they loved the do-it-yourself fashion accessories," said Rarity.

"It just doesn't make any sense," Fluttershy whispered.

"Unless," said Applejack, "the Great and Powerful Trixie is getting mixed up in this in some way—"

"No," interrupted Sunset Shimmer. "This isn't Trixie's fault."

While her friends had been talking, Sunset Shimmer had been looking around the cafeteria, and what she saw had shown her what was going on. Kids were stealing sideways glances at her and then whispering and pointing at her. She was the gossip of the cafeteria. She'd been so happy to make things right with her friends that she had forgotten that the whole rest of the school had only seen the trouble she had made—the chaotic kitchen, the runaway rescues, and what must have looked like mean photos of Rarity on their fan site. To make sure that she was right, Sunset Shimmer got up to throw her trash in the garbage can. As she walked back to her table, she overheard what the kids were saying.

"Who knows what she's planning this time? I just don't want to be there...."

"I've heard she's called back the Sirens and they are going to take over the whole school."

"But didn't she help defeat them?"

"You never know...."

"What's she going to do to our school this time?"

"Is there any way to stop her?"

"Just don't go to that fashion show. Stay home!"

Sunset Shimmer slumped back into her seat. "I'm sorry, everyone. This is all my fault. I'm not a pony anymore, and every time I try to be a real girl, I mess it up. I'm a failure at everything." She put her head in her hands, defeated.

Her friends tried to console her, but just as they were trying to reassure her that everything would be all right, Principal Celestia dropped by their table. "I just want to say, girls, that you really seem to have pulled this together. I'm proud of you. I really am."

Sunset Shimmer shook her head. "But she's going to be so disappointed when she sees that empty auditorium. And it's all my fault. All I've done is create another school-wide disaster."

"I think we've got to advertise that new song you said you were going to write for us," said Pinkie Pie. "No one will be able to resist that."

Sunset Shimmer gulped, remembering her promise at the sleepover. She had totally forgotten about the song. She smiled weakly. "Right. The new song. I'll come up with something. But that still doesn't solve the problem of how suspicious everyone is of me."

"We'll figure out something," said Fluttershy.

"We always do," agreed Applejack.

Sunset Shimmer shook her head. "I don't think so. I think this time I've just gone too far."

"Nonsense!" Pinkie Pie perked up. "Everyone wants to come to the fashion show. You know they do! Music! Animals! Fashion! What's the problem? What we have to do is just find some way to get people excited about it again. They want to be excited."

Sunset Shimmer looked at Pinkie Pie with amazement. Nothing ever spoiled her day. She was a ray of bubblegum-colored sunshine, always eager to look at the bright side of things and make everyone happy. What a gift she had. How could Sunset Shimmer have ever imagined that there was any more powerful magic than that?

Pinkie Pie was rattling off a list of ideas. "We could throw a raffle and offer a free concert to the person who wins. Or we could promise some big surprise, but we'd have to figure out what it was. Or maybe we just need more balloons!"

The girls were putting their heads together.

"I like the raffle idea," said Applejack.

"But will it work?" wondered Rainbow Dash.

Sunset Shimmer cleared her throat. "No," she said. "That's not what we need to do. In fact, the rest of you have done enough already. This is up to me. I'm the one who has to prove to everyone that I'm not up to something dangerous. That's what they're scared of—me. And the only way I can prove to them that I'm different now is to show them. I've got to do it the same way that I've showed all of you. I wish I had more than an afternoon to do it in, but there it is."

"Mighty big of you," said Applejack.

"Mighty brave of you," said Fluttershy.

"You think it will work?" asked Rarity.

Pinkie Pie clapped her hands. "Of course it will! I think Sunset Shimmer can do anything, and I think it's going to be wonderful!"

Pinkie Pie's optimism was just what Sunset Shimmer needed.

CHAPTER

14

With Flying Colors

★ ★ ★

When Sunset Shimmer stood up, she felt everyone's eyes on her. She realized that if she did anything showy, kids would say that she was just pretending to be nice or, even worse, up to something. Whatever she did, it had to happen naturally—that was the way Rainbow Dash was at her best, and she would just have to trust, the way Pinkie Pie did, that the rest of the day would offer her opportunities to show the whole school that she wasn't power-hungry anymore.

And it did.

On her way to class from lunch, she saw a girl standing in front of her locker. An avalanche of papers, books, and pencils had fallen out of it. Everything that should have been in her locker was on the floor.

"Here," said Sunset Shimmer, rushing over. "Let me help you with that."

The girl gasped and jumped back, clearly frightened.

But Sunset Shimmer collected her books and papers and handed them to her. "There. My locker gets like that this time of year, too."

Sunset Shimmer walked off down the

hallway. She was tempted to look back, but she didn't. If this was going to work, she was going to have to trust in the real magic of friendship. That didn't involve plotting and planning, shortcuts, and second-guessing. It just meant being a good friend.

Kids cleared a path for Sunset Shimmer in the hallway, and she kept her head down, trying to focus on people who needed her help. This was going to take time, step by step, just like baking. She was about to go into math class when she heard a quiet sob from the stairwell. Someone was crying. Who could it be?

Sunset Shimmer was stunned to discover the Great and Powerful Trixie sitting on the steps with tearstained cheeks. "What's the matter?" she asked, walking over.

"Nothing!" said Trixie, collecting herself. "Nothing at all."

"Really?" persisted Sunset Shimmer. "It doesn't look that way."

"It's just that I thought there was going to be all this drama again."

Sunset Shimmer nodded, listening carefully. "Why would you want that?" she asked.

"Well, I thought maybe you'd stop being friends with the Sonic Rainbooms, and, well, then you and I could team up...."

"You've been spreading rumors about me so that nobody wants to come to the fashion show," realized Sunset Shimmer.

Trixie shrugged. "Maybe."

Sunset Shimmer sat down beside Trixie. "I'd like to be friends with you, Trixie. You've got a lot of energy. You really do. It's kind of amazing. But I'm also friends with the Sonic

Rainbooms. After all, they've stayed friends with me despite everything I've done."

Trixie sniffed.

No one ever wanted to feel left out. Trixie didn't. Sunset Shimmer didn't. With a start, she realized there were lots of kids who had a hard time finding their place in school and making friends. Maybe the way Fluttershy helped rescue pets, she could help people who needed a friend—even if it was just someone to sit with at lunch or invite to a sleepover. Maybe the best way to learn about friendship was being friends with all different kinds of people.

"Hey, I have an idea," Sunset Shimmer suggested. "Why don't you help us with the fashion show tonight?"

Trixie brightened. "Really? What can I do?"

Sunset Shimmer smiled. "We do need help getting more people to come tonight. Ticket sales haven't been great...."

"I can sell tickets!" exclaimed Trixie.

"Yeah!" said Sunset Shimmer. "Thank you so much." She gave Trixie a big hug before dashing off to math class just before the door closed.

She slipped into the desk right beside Flash Sentry. He was erasing something on a work sheet. Poor Flash! He struggled in math class.

"Hey, Flash," she whispered. "You want any help with that problem?"

Flash shook his head. He was just like everyone else. He didn't trust her. Could she blame him?

It wasn't right to give him the answer. That was show-offy. What could she do?

Maybe he just needed a little bit of help, a hint, and then he could figure it out on his own. "Try subtracting the three," she whispered.

"What? Oh!" Flash's eyes widened. "I get it! Thank you, Sunset Shimmer."

"You're welcome, Flash." Maybe he wasn't so bad at math after all. He figured that out pretty fast. "You don't have any advice about songwriting, by any chance, do you?"

"Songwriting?"

"Yeah, I've got to come up with some lyrics for a new song."

"Just have fun!"

"That's what Pinkie Pie would say."

"Pinkie Pie's usually right," said Flash.

The rest of Sunset Shimmer's day was filled with good deeds and simple friendliness.

By the time the bell rang, Sunset

Shimmer thought she would be exhausted. But she wasn't. Her classes had sped by, and each simple act of kindness had given her a little jolt of energy. She was the first of the Sonic Rainbooms to get to the auditorium. Still, she didn't have a song yet—and she didn't know how to write one.

Dear Twilight Sparkle, she wrote. *Do you have any advice about writing a song? How can I have fun when I do it?*

An answer appeared instantaneously. *Just remember you don't have to win any competitions. You don't have to be the best songwriter or write a hit tune. What do you really want? You want to make sure you show you've changed.*

That was it, realized Sunset Shimmer. She'd just tell everyone that she'd grown since she first got to Canterlot High—and that was easy.

Sunset pulled out a note Rarity had slipped into her locker earlier. As she unfolded the paper, she revealed elaborate dress designs. Rarity was designing something special just for Sunset's performance. Sunset felt loved—and like she belonged.

"What are you doing in here all by yourself?" asked Rainbow Dash, sitting down beside her. "You ready to jam?"

"I am!" Sunset Shimmer laughed. "And I think I've got my song ready. Have you heard how the tickets are selling?"

"Not a clue," said Rainbow Dash. "We'll find out tonight. Although Trixie and Pinkie Pie together make a pretty convincing team. I don't think anyone was allowed to get on the bus without buying one."

After she finished laughing, Sunset

Shimmer turned to Rainbow Dash. "Can I ask you a question?"

"Anything," Rainbow Dash answered promptly.

Sunset Shimmer took a breath. "This whole week you didn't say one mean thing to me. It's not that I nearly ruined the fashion show, I nearly ruined your team's chances for new uniforms."

"But it was your idea in the first place to have the fashion show. Your first instinct was to do something good for your friends. You've got a good heart, Sunset Shimmer."

"Really?" Sunset Shimmer was very surprised.

"Yep," said Rainbow Dash. "It's just hard sometimes to find your place on the team. To know how best to play your position. If you know what I mean."

"But I don't have any special talents like the rest of you...."

"Isn't being a friend the most special thing of all? Being on a team is not about being a star—it's about working together."

No wonder all the kids on the soccer team looked up to Rainbow Dash. It wasn't because she was the best kicker or got the most goals. No. It was because she was loyal to the team itself. She knew it took a team to win the game. She valued every player. She was loyal.

Rainbow Dash stood up. "Help me set up the amps? It's time to rock our new uniforms!"

"Absolutely," said Sunset Shimmer. "There's nothing I want to do more in the whole world!"

Sunset Shimmer Shines

★ ★ ★

Sunset Shimmer peeked out from behind the curtains. The audience was beginning to fill up! Out in the lobby, Pinkie Pie and Trixie were collecting tickets and Applejack was selling donuts. Backstage, Rarity was helping the athletes get into their uniforms to model them. Fluttershy was tying the last bows and ribbons on the kittens and puppies. Rainbow Dash was checking on the amps and tuning her guitar.

Sunset Shimmer had been very busy this last hour. She had run to the cafeteria to find the paper cups for Applejack's cider. She had soothed a nervous kitten. She had helped set up the band's equipment. When she realized that there was nothing else she could do, she checked her journal and saw it glowing. Twilight Sparkle had written her.

I am so proud of you, Sunset Shimmer. I know this past week hasn't been easy, but you haven't given up, and I think you will find as the days pass that there is even more magic to friendship than you can possibly imagine. Who knows what surprises are in store for you? Your friend always and forever, Twilight Sparkle

Sunset Shimmer held her journal close. It was almost as if the magic glow radiated right into her heart. She felt warm and happy. What would she have done without Twilight Sparkle? She hoped that someday she could be as helpful to someone else as the Princess of Friendship had been to her.

DJ Pon-3 was spinning some discs as the audience got settled. Rainbow Dash hurried over to Sunset Shimmer and noticed the full auditorium.

"That's a lot of tickets!" exclaimed Sunset Shimmer.

"That's a whole new set of soccer uniforms!" Rainbow Dash was beaming. "Think we should dim the lights soon?"

"Whenever you're ready," said Sunset Shimmer.

Rainbow Dash squeezed Sunset Shimmer's hand. "Thank you for everything," she whispered.

The glow in Sunset Shimmer's heart was even brighter.

As they lined up for their turn on the runway, the athletes were comparing their decals.

"I chose a pony!"

"I've got a rainbow!"

"I put a sunset on mine," exclaimed one girl, "because we owe our new uniforms to Sunset Shimmer."

Sunset Shimmer blushed. "It was teamwork," she said. "Lots of teamwork."

The audience cheered and applauded as the athletes modeled their new look. The music blasted. A disco ball filled the auditorium with sparkly lights. After the soccer team and the field hockey girls paraded, Fluttershy's animals wiggled and wobbled in their adorable outfits down the runway.

"They are too sweet!" said someone in the audience.

"Oh, I want a kitten," announced one of the soccer players.

"Me too!"

"Me too!"

Fluttershy couldn't believe it. At intermission, everyone was coming up to her in the lobby and asking how they could adopt new pets from the shelter. When she had a free moment, Fluttershy gave Sunset Shimmer a hug. "I just thought this would be a good way to raise money for the sports teams. I didn't realize it was going to help the animals find homes. What a night you've helped us create, Sunset Shimmer."

"That sure is the truth!" said Applejack. "I've sold every treat. Every one! Best bake sale ever!"

"All right, girls," said Pinkie Pie, bouncing over. "The hard work of the night is done and it's time to rock! You girls ready to sing?"

"Yes!" they shouted together.

* * *

As the group headed toward the stage, Rarity pulled Sunset aside.

"You'll simply shine in this," Rarity said as she handed Sunset a garment bag.

Sunset gasped as she unzipped it to reveal a stunningly gorgeous dress.

Rarity beamed. "We don't have much time before curtain! Let me help you into it."

* * *

Behind the closed curtain, the girls took their places. Rainbow Dash picked up her guitar. Applejack tuned her bass, and Rarity positioned her fingers over her keytar. Pinkie Pie was on the drums. Fluttershy had her tambourine, and Sunset Shimmer was ready to sing backup harmonies. Only she'd discovered that she liked hearing her voice blend with the voices of her friends. She really did.

The lights dimmed. The audience became quiet. The curtains opened, and Rarity strummed her guitar.

"We're all different,
But our music is the same.
It's the sound of friendship.

It's in the rhythm of our names.
Fluttershy listens and never drops a beat.
Pinkie Pie's tempo keeps you tapping your feet.
Rarity's playing keeps us all in tune,
And Sunset's vocals shimmer over the moon.
Applejack's notes make you want to sing,
And, Rainbow Dash, she riffs on everything!"

As each girl's name was sung, she began to pony up. First ears appeared and then manes and finally tails. They pranced and danced as the magic took over. The audience was singing along and swaying from side to side. The disco ball was turning. The lights were glittering. But as the girls' voices reached their final harmonies, something else happened in the auditorium.

"Ooooh!"

"Aahhhh!"

"Wow!"

Tiny, sparkling rainbows were gently falling from the ceiling like snowflakes. Each one was a perfect shimmering arch of joyous colors. It was like enchanted butterflies had filled the room. What a special effect! How had the girls done it?

The audience rose to their feet, applauding. What a show!

"Encore! Encore! Encore!" they yelled.

The Sonic Rainbooms played song after song late into the night. When, finally, the curtain came down for the last time, the girls looked at one another, exhausted and amazed.

"What happened?" asked Sunset Shimmer, awed.

"It was the Magic of Friendship," said Rainbow Dash.

And it was.

Over the Rainbow

★ ★ ★

Sunset Shimmer was soon very busy at Canterlot High. She tried out for the soccer team and joined the school newspaper. She volunteered at Fluttershy's animal shelter and began offering free math tutoring on the weekends. But most of all, she was busy with her friends. She had discovered that her special talent was being helpful.

There were photos to share and movies to go to and pizza parties and band practices and talking on the phone and texting all day long and gossiping at their lockers. The days flew by, and sometimes in the midst of giggling with Pinkie Pie or baking with Applejack, Sunset Shimmer would see a momentary cascade of the same rainbows that had filled the auditorium during the fashion show.

As a former student of magic, she couldn't help feeling just a little curious about them. One night at a slumber party, the girls were all working on a new song together. Pinkie Pie was experimenting with a syncopated beat. Rainbow Dash was trying out a melody, and Rarity and

Applejack were singing harmony. Sunset Shimmer's voice joined theirs, and she lost herself in the music. There it was. A little rainbow. Just for a second. Sometimes she wondered if she was the only one who saw them. Maybe they were just a reminder to her of how the Magic of Friendship really happened.

"What are you thinking?" Fluttershy asked Sunset Shimmer.

Sunset Shimmer smiled. "I'm thinking that I'm lucky to have such good friends."

"Me too," said Applejack.

But later that night when all the girls had settled down, Sunset Shimmer took out her journal. *Dear Twilight Sparkle,* she wrote. *A lot has changed in my life because, when it comes to friendship, there's a lot to learn and a lot to practice. Every day I discover something* new about what it means to be a good friend. I have been wondering, however, about these little rainbows that appear sometimes. Sometimes they happen when we are singing and sometimes they happen when we are having a good time together. What kind of magic are they? Are they the same kind of magic as ponying up? Is there anything I should know about them? Just curious.

In an instant, the journal began glowing and Twilight Sparkle's response appeared.

Dear Sunset Shimmer, Sometimes the magic really does happen, but you don't have to understand everything. Just be grateful for it, as I'm sure you are. Your friend, Twilight Sparkle

Sunset Shimmer put down her journal. She was grateful for the magic, for the friendship, for everything that had happened to her. Still. There's nothing wrong with being curious, is there? she wrote back.

The words materialized on the page. *Careful, Sunset Shimmer! Careful!*

✶ ✶ ✶

Back in Equestria, Twilight Sparkle shook her head and laughed a little. "I'll just have to hope those girls keep Sunset Shimmer busy. Very busy."

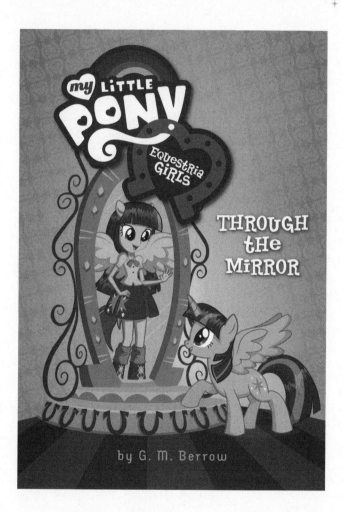

Turn the page for a sneak peek of
Equestria Girls: Through the Mirror.

The
Princess Summit

★ ★ ★

The castle of the Crystal Empire sparkled brilliantly in the midday sun. Ponies pranced around the Kingdom, running their daily errands in the market or playing outside in the gorgeous weather. In fact, everypony was so busy that they didn't notice that seven visitors from afar had just arrived through the front gate. It was six ponies and one small dragon, to be exact.

The recently crowned Princess Twilight Sparkle trotted along with her friends, pulling her suitcase behind her and taking in the dazzling scene. She loved visiting her brother's kingdom—this must have been her fourth or fifth visit so far! But for once, it wasn't because somepony needed saving!

This time, Twilight was here for another reason, and of course, her best friends had insisted on being there to support her. Okay, and maybe to sample a few Crystal berry tarts or check out the Equestria Games stadium if there was time. Either way, it was comforting to have her best ponies there with her.

"Whoo-ee! Your very first Princess Summit. You must be over the moon, Twilight!"

exclaimed Applejack, turning to her royal friend. Twilight Sparkle had taken up the lead, as royal ponies were known to do. Twilight furrowed her brow in concern and looked back at her crew.

"Well, I *am* excited. But, to be honest..." Twilight stalled, then admitted, "I'm a little nervous, too." Twilight hadn't been a princess for very long, after all. Even after everything she'd learned from Princess Cadance and the Crystal Heart Spell, she still felt that there was much more to discover every day. Twilight just hoped she would have *something* to contribute to the Princess Summit.

Pinkie Pie trotted up to join them, a wide smile on her face and an extra bounce in her prance. "You're just *nervicited*!" Her curly fuchsia mane bounced wildly as she spoke. "It's like you want to jump up and down and yell, 'Yay me!'" She took a soaring leap into the air. A ray of sunlight glinted against her pearly white smile and sparkled. All of a sudden, she became serious and her face fell. "But you also want to curl up in a teeny-tiny ball and hide at the same time!" Pinkie fell to the ground and curled herself up, rocking back and forth.

Rarity and Rainbow Dash exchanged a skeptical look at the dramatic display before Pinkie Pie popped back up and patted Twilight reassuringly. "Don't worry, Twilight. We've all been there," Pinkie said knowingly.

Fluttershy, who had floated into the air for a moment to stretch her pale yellow wings, landed gracefully on the ground. "I'm there almost every day," she agreed in her soft voice. Up front, Twilight Sparkle took in her surroundings with just the slightest trace of hesitation. Even though she had visited the Empire several times before, the first glimpse of the Crystal Castle always stirred something inside her. It was just so big and beautiful. And intimidating. She took a deep breath and kept walking.

Applejack, who was trotting right beside her, noticed Twilight's frown. She was just about to toss a few more comforting words the princess's way when Rarity gasped in shock, stopping all six ponies in their tracks. "Sorry, darlings, but I just noticed that Twilight's not wearing her crown!" Rarity was always shocked that Twilight still felt self-conscious about wearing it.

"Don't worry, Rarity," Twilight assured her. "It's safe here in my bag."

"But you're attending a Princess Summit!

I'm telling you, if I had a gorgeous crown like that I'd never take it off!" Rarity exclaimed. "Why, I'd sleep in the thing."

As soon as Twilight and her friends entered the foyer of the Crystal Castle, her nerves began to melt away like ice cream on a warm summer day. The Empire was starting to feel a little more like a home away from home to her. Twilight attempted to hold her head high in order to give off an air of confidence to anypony who might be watching, but the sound of royal trumpets suddenly blared through the castle. Twilight was startled by the loud racket and stumbled. Unfortunately, being a princess didn't automatically make a pony graceful.

"Ooof!" Twilight grunted as she braced herself on the chest of a handsome Crystal Royal Guard with a bright blue mane. He leaned forward to help her regain her balance with a small smile on his face. Then he remembered his duty and immediately snapped back to attention in time to announce her arrival.

"Her Highness, Princess Twilight Sparkle!" he projected his voice into the echoey Crystal corridor. Twilight blushed a little more than usual at the attention, though she didn't know why. It's not like she even knew this particular royal guard pony.

Nearby, Pinkie smiled wide with delight at all the pomp and circumstance. It just so happened that she loved pomp and also circumstance. But *together*—they were superduper fun!

Suddenly, Princess Cadance, Princess Luna, and Princess Celestia delicately trotted up to meet the six ponies and Spike.

The ponies of the Crystal Royal Guard straightened themselves to appear even taller than before.

Cadance smiled warmly. Her pink-and-purple mane cascaded into soft waves around her face, and she wore her own shimmering golden tiara so confidently, it seemed like it was a part of her. Maybe someday Twilight would, too. "Twilight! It's been so long since I've seen you!" Cadance nuzzled her young sister-in-law.

Princess Celestia stepped forward to join them, looking just as elegant and regal as the young princesses. Her pastel mane and tail flowed behind her. "We have so much to discuss. But it can wait until tomorrow. You all look tired from your journey." A quick glance at the pack of weary travelers was enough to confirm that she was right. Applejack, Rainbow Dash, and Fluttershy all had dark circles forming under their eyes. Rarity's mane was looking a bit frizzy. And Pinkie Pie was twitching a little bit. But that could have been from excitement—it was hard to tell with her.

The ponies nodded in agreement and happily accepted Celestia's invitation to make their way to the guest quarters of the castle. As they hoofed their way down the hallway, their eyelids drooped with the heavy weight of sleep. Rarity was the only pony who remained alert—but that was just because she couldn't help but gawk at every gem and crystal encrusted in the archways and window frames. It was the type of decor she'd always envisioned herself living with.

It was really too bad that the friends were all either too dazzled or sleepy to notice that somepony was nearby. Somepony who was hiding in the shadows and watching their every move. Somepony who wanted to remain hidden.

✶ ✶ ✶

Being the pony she was, Twilight couldn't go to sleep until all her belongings were unpacked and stowed away safely in the appropriate places. There had to be a certain order to things, whether she was at home in Ponyville or not. Routines helped her to feel like the same old Twilight she'd always been. Twilight's purple Unicorn horn glowed as she used her magic to put each item from her suitcase folded in a drawer, hung in the wardrobe, or placed on the bookshelf. (She'd packed only a couple of books.) Spike watched with mild interest, his attention being tested by the abundance of jewels everywhere. His gem-hoarding dragon instincts were starting to take over.

Twilight lifted the princess crown from her bag and tried to position it on her head. The delicate gold tiara supported a shimmering magenta gemstone—an Element of Harmony, a very powerful stone infused with Magic. But instead of looking pretty like Cadance's, the shining tiara dipped awkwardly down to one side, smushing Twilight's bangs. One look at her reflection confirmed Twilight's anxieties. She was no princess, and here she was at the Princess Summit! A summit of princesses!

"What's wrong, Twilight?" asked Spike, suddenly snapping out of his daydream about a peanut butter and *jewelly* sandwich.

The crown slipped a little farther down

Twilight's face. It was no use. It floated up off her head as she used her horn to magically put it down gently on a table. "I'm just…worried, I guess. Princess Cadance was given the Crystal Empire to rule over. What if now that I'm a princess, Celestia expects me to lead a kingdom of my own?" Twilight stared at the crown, sitting lonely on a small, ornate table by her bed.

Spike marveled at the idea of *his* Twilight running a kingdom. Maybe she'd make him into some royal advisor or better yet— jewel commissioner. "That. Would. Be. Awesome."

Twilight frowned. "No. It wouldn't!" She began to pace around. "Just because I have this crown and these new wings, it doesn't mean I'd be a good leader."

"Sure, you would," Spike said, using his

last ounce of energy to cheer up his best friend. A wave of exhaustion washed over him. "Now come on. You should get some shut-eye. Big day tomorrow!" And with that, he crawled into the tiny bed that was set up next to Twilight's and made himself snug in his blanket. A short moment later, he was fast asleep, sucking on his claw.

It wasn't so easy for the new princess, however. She was absolutely desperate to find a comfortable position in which to rest her new wings. For the next ten minutes, she squirmed and stretched. She rolled and reached. She wiggled and wormed. Twilight had never realized how much work the feathery things could be! As she twisted around in her bed, Twilight made a mental note to discuss optimal wing-sleeping positions with Fluttershy and Rainbow Dash in the morning. Finally, she found a good spot. *That's better,* she thought, closing her eyes at last.

Sproing! Suddenly, her left wing popped out of the covers. Twilight sighed heavily. Apparently, there were a lot of things about her new life that were going to take some getting used to—summits, wings, and crowns were only the start. But, hey, at least she didn't have to sleep in her crown.

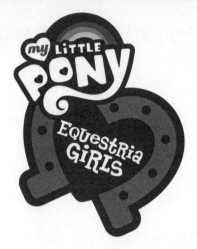

THe MaGiC of FRieNDSHiP

Sunset Shimmer is learning some
important lessons about how to be a good
friend—and Twilight Sparkle, the Princess
of Friendship, helps guide her.
Turn the page to explore the Magic
of Friendship with the Equestria Girls!

THe POWeR of PeN PaLS

Sunset Shimmer and Twilight Sparkle use a magic journal to exchange letters. If you could write to Twilight Sparkle, what would you ask her about friendship? Use the form below to send your first letter!

Dear Twilight Sparkle,

My friends are _____

_____.

Our favorite things to do together are _____

_____ and _____.

Our favorite movie is _____,

and our favorite song is _____.

The best memory that we share is the time that we _____

_____.

I have one question about friendship: _____

_____?

Your new friend,

_____

WHAT MAKES YOU SHINE?

Pinkie Pie decorates pillows for all
her friends with pictures of what makes
them special. Color in each girl's decal—and
then create a decal that shows one of
your favorite things or activities!

Fun at the Fund-Raiser

Canterlot High is raising money for new team uniforms with a fashion show. If you were a friend of the Equestria Girls, how would you help out? In what special way could you contribute? Brainstorm a list of all your ideas on how YOU could make a difference!

_____

_____

_____

_____

_____

_____

_____

_____

Rays of Sunshine

What makes each of your friends special?
Create your very own yearbook
to celebrate them!

Name:
Fluttershy

Special Interest or Talent:
Animals

Friendship Magic:
Listening

Name:
_____

Special Interest or Talent:
_____

Friendship Magic:
_____

Name:
_____

Special Interest or Talent:
_____

Friendship Magic:
_____

Match the Magic

Sunset Shimmer discovers that each of the Equestria Girls understands something important about friendship. Match each friend with her special friendship skill.

Listening

Honesty

Teamwork

Optimism

Celebrating Differences

What makes you a good friend?
What is your special friendship magic?